SHH PURELY POETRY

Sensual, Love and
Relationship Poems

M J Mallon

Kyrosmagica Publishing

SHH PURELY POETRY

Sensual, Love and
Relationship Poems

permission from the author. The only exception is by a reviewer who may quote short excerpts for a review. Thank you for your support of this author's rights.

This book is to be available via The British Library.

Published in kindle, and also in paperback: ISBN: 978-1-9998224-8-4

mjmallon.com

Cover Design by: M J Mallon

Photography: background cover image created on Canva, line drawing of girl by Victoria Rusyn.

CONTENTS

DEDICATION

I Whispered My Love is dedicated to my husband.
Love Has No Age is dedicated to my mum and dad.

To all those that seek love.
To all those that have found love.
Hold love dear in your hearts.
Stoke its many coloured flame.
Keep it glowing, keep it burning!

LOVE IS FUEL

BREAKFAST NIBBLES

Avocado spread on toast,
Like her bikini, green, shiny, lush,
Skimpy but oh, so satisfying!

Full breakfast, or bacon roll?
Depends on afters...
Your place or mine?

Warm veggie sausage,
Sizzles on a hotplate,
Orange juice, saucy smiles.

Bacon buttie,
Crisp and inviting,
Hot tea, sparkling eyes!

Roti Chana, can't say no.
Curry dip, taste buds tingle.
Ought to spice things up!

Pancakes with maple syrup,
A sweet tooth,
We share the same spoon.

Eggs sunny side up,

Or easy over,
I scramble over beside you.

Griddled scones,
With brown speckles,
Like your freckles.

Oatmeal overnight,
Stay at mine, love,
Breakfast and back rubs.

Cream of wheat,
Honey for two,
Darling taste this!

Bran flakes, sultanas,
Apples, bananas,
Splash of milk. Nibble nibble!

Fruit salad, yogurt,
Low cal to be skinny,
To squeeze into our single bed!

DINING ON POETRY

Let us dine on poetry,
Eat words of love,
And entwine together.
In the divine.

Leaning towards me he pulls me close.
Feeling his proximity hurts me.
I can't breathe.
When his lips touch mine,
I forget everything.
Everything but the pressure of his lips.
The sweetness.
The longing.
Each kiss is deeper.
Different and the same.
Like I belonged to more than him.
Like I belonged to the poetry.

The notebook has never known ink.

Its pages are pristine.

Write! I command.

He grabs his hair and stabs the page.

Tears spill from his eyes.

As he write a single word: you.

We hug, our tears mingling with raindrops.

The thunder calms.

I know what to call you.

Mine, we both whisper.

And then we kiss.

The kiss is so poetic.

We will never be alone again.

COFFEE - THROAT PUNCH

Coffee. Aphrodisiac. Arsenal of choice.
Almighty stimulant.

Who dares to say don't?
Don't drink.
Strict instructions given.
Total abstinence from!
For a least an hour after your visit.

Must be adhered to.
No Throat Punch.

Oh, and no sex, not ever.
Not until you have brushed and flossed your teeth!

Must be adhered to. No Throat Punch.

Dentists and their tortuous taboos!

***

Throat punch isn't a cocktail served
in laced up boxing gloves,
with a colourful paper-thin umbrella.

Neither is it an alcoholic remedy for sore throats,
or a weird euphemism for rough sex.

Throat punch tickles the tonsils.
Its warm aroma invites togetherness.
Conjuring up illicit, passionate liaisons.
It stimulates sensory satisfaction, with mighty
mind fuel discover coffee granule magic!

Such genius. Imagine - the coffee lovers in situ.

Hear the raucous laughter in the room.
Feel the smiles. The flow of the coffee love
as it invites mysterious strangers to sip mochas.
While long time lovers fall headlong
rippling the surface of flat white after flat white.

Festival performers show off lick cappuccinos
with carefully constructed chocolate hearts.
Their perfection, too perfect to destroy.
Lovers steal stolen sweet kiss after sweet kiss.

Before gulping extra strength espresso shots.

The coffee love grows, its divine force
remains unchallenged.
No one debates the need for a double

shot of wake-up fuel.
Not until we need another punch.

The alcoholic kind which we must choose ourselves.

HOT SHOWER POUNDING PETALS ON MY SKIN

Splish splash splosh the water goes plop.
Hot shower pounding petals on my skin.
Downstairs, towel dried, hair up.
I roam hearing pitter, patter,
waking up neighbour sounds.
These walls are staccato thin!
Clitter clatter clang, pot lids bash.
Rat a tat tat, a knock at my door.
Ignore it, too early for that!

Flip flop a curtain flaps.
A neighbour grunts, groans, grumbles,
drips, incoherently, his verbal faucet forced open.

A typical day, I yawn, gawping, stretching.
See where the kettle is, me bleary-eyed
First cup of tea slurped and supped.
A new day begins, time to crunch some toast.

Where will this day take me? Somewhere sweet?

Toast spread scraping butter
lashes and special preserve raspberry jam.
Flavours waking me up, taste buds tingling.
Making me gasp in unashamed delight!

VALENTINE'S IN CHOCOLATES

Valentine's in chocolates,
I can still feel her lips on mine,
Salty like the caramel snack.
That she turned down for peanuts.

My hands caress her breasts.
They sit up pert.
Asking - no begging to be touched.

Her stomach, an exquisite ride.
Down, down to the sweetest prize.
Her cherry bonbon nestled, in
between the welcoming spot of her thighs.

Damn it tastes so good,
knowing what' s coming.

This climax.
An explosion.
Of my lovesick juices.

THE SUMMER & WINTER OF LOVE

MY HONEY DEAREST
MY SWEETEST YOU

Yellow, a splash of brilliant colour
Between green and orange
That bright luminous dress
Mesmerising memories
All those years ago when we first met
Our light, carefree, sparkling smiles
Sunny, fun days, us two by the beach
Lazing on the warm sand, laughing
Sending yellow smiley emojis
And each day a new surprise for you
Today, my smiley face bikini
Hidden beneath my yellow dress
My tiny tummy ready for our shared lunch
A crunchy corncob on a barbeque
That blessed burger in a yellow brioche bun
Followed by homemade French vanilla ice cream
Made with love's lightest yellow egg yolks
Midday heat bringing thirsty, tantalising, thoughts

A golden Mojito, or a lemon drop martini?
Such a perfect day, and now so mellow
Oh, the promise of sunflower days, ardent
nights and tangy dreams.
How I miss you, how I do.
Wish you were here with me, my love.
My honey, dearest, my sweetest you!

TANGERINE DRESS

You wore a tangerine dress the day I met you
On the beach we sat on the sand
Your citrine necklace completed you
Your positively shone like the sun
I swam peeking in and out of the coral
Feeling like this nobody by your side
As you splashed and squealed
I wished to become a better version of you
A carnelian to boost my self esteem
Must wear it, to make it work
Enhance my flagging energy
I'd no longer be this jealous girl
Hiding amongst the tiny fish
Instead, I'd be all colour and laughter
Crimson heart bursting full and complete
My lips bright as aubergine-coloured kisses
My brilliance overshadowing yours!

MY WARM SANDCASTLE

My warm sandcastle, playing with you,
makes my heartbeat faster.
Covering your breasts and body
I leave your heart exposed.

It's warm this saucy, sunny day.
You giggle with delicious delight.
Your shoulders urge release.
Come here, I am ready!

Broken free from your restraints
you pull me down upon you.
Sand in our hair, ears, mouth.
And every which where too!

The waves ride slick and low.
Upon our salty seashell bed.
The sea storms with secrets.
Rocking our bodies back and forth.

Splish, splash, splosh,
Love is here, glance away!
Oh, what a joy, the sea rides upon us.
Withdraws. Returns. Rejoice!

BEACH ROCKS

These beach rocks remind me of you
Glimmering smooth and divine
Your chiselled form tempts me
Willing me to be brave I get a grip
But fear I will trip, stumble and fall
So, I wind my way ever so gently
Tiptoeing with eyes shut tight
My touch alone becoming my eyes
Confidence grows with each step
Feeling for the perfect point
Gripping your hard surface, I sigh.
Hardly able to breathe
Overcome with aching adrenalin
I suck in a breath letting it blow out slowly
What a rush to be here, to be now
Delightfully aware, at the summit of us.

OUR LOG CABIN
CHRISTMAS GETAWAY

Our log cabin in the winter woods
Is covered so deep in snow.
It is inaccessible.
Unearthed only by snowploughs.

Our log cabin in the winter woods.
Is our place to be together.
To discover each other again.
In winter's sublime tranquillity.

Our log cabin in the winter woods.
Has twinkling brilliant lights.
A real Christmas tree.
And unwrapped gifts.

Our log cabin in the winter woods.
Is our place to be.
In love every Christmas.
Just us two.

MY FIRST GLIMPSE OF
THE CHRISTMAS TREE

My first glimpse of the Christmas tree
It makes us wonder you and me
Holds my heart full with such gladness
I laugh you smile.

Off to dinner and all the while
So many sights are there, enjoy
My first glimpse of the Christmas tree
I laugh you smile.

Twinkling lights both near and afar
This magic moment shared we two
A pattern in the river twirls
I laugh you smile.

LOST LOVE
DISCOVERING LOVE

THE TREE OF LOST LOVE

Under a Mallorcan tree
Holding hands, we kissed and sighed
And deeper, deepest, we fell in love.
Now that tree is one of many.
Newly planted they grow and thrive.
Each year I find it again.
Weeping I lament our lost love.
Gathering its roots towards me
I become its bark.

BLOOMS OF BLOSSOMING BLISS

Fragility of your flame
Memories not lost
Recalled by raindrops falling
Caressing tender petals

Incorrigible thoughts
Lingering taste of kisses
Pale skin blushing pink
Desire strengthening

Reaching out to discover
The soul of each other
Embracing in the mist
Blooms of blossoming bliss.

© Melissa Davilio, & M J Mallon

HIS GIRLFRIEND'S
LONG WHITE COAT

A lone white swan floats
Moving slow in reflections
Upon still water, no boats.
This day out surprises
A girl on her boyfriend dotes.
Tranquil scene amid sculptural park
Boy's admiring behaviour, in love connotes.
Tender movements, in gentle affections
Buttoning his girlfriend's long white coat.

THE UNIVERSE IS OURS

The universe is ours, you said.
Looking up at the stars
Two astronauts in space
Moon walking
Floating apart
Losing sight of each other
I willed you to come closer
But you kept on floating away
I imagined you next to me
Holding my hand
Keeping me warm and close
As we landed
You lifted my astronaut visor
And planted a kiss on my lips
It was like yesterday
The kiss still tingling
But nothing is the same
You are now a particle
Taken by the universe
Forever roaming

Loving the moon
More than me.

LOVE PLUCKED

The night sky should be filled with stars
But I can only find two.

I gaze at them from here afar
The lonely night ensues.

If only I could turn back time.
To find that sparkle we once had.
To hold you close, to see the
moon and stardust trails with you.

If only I could wrangle comets
I'd store them up in jars.
To give you just as I promised.
My love plucked from the stars.

© A. Lee Wells & M J Mallon

LOVE HIDDEN IN
THE MARGINS

if i were a poem
i'd grace a beautiful notebook
its cover bright sunflowers
inside a ray of sunshine.

beautiful calligraphy to highlight
tiny ink splodges to add character
tear drops to remind me of sad days
poems of sunshine and sadness
grief and joy. life and loves.
funny poems. nonsense poems.
all manner of poems.

torn pages, folded memories.
crisp, pristine fragments
forgotten dreams
edges filled with notes
synonyms and rhyme schemes.
if I were a poem

i'd close my eyes, meditate,
light a candle,

and write one just for you.
on the last page you'll find it.
hidden in the margins,
in our secret language
saying how much I love you.

(Love Hidden in The Margins first appeared
in Today Magazine, Portugal.)

TRIBUTE POETRY – I CHERISH YOUR SWEET SOUL

This poem is inspired by E E. CUMMINGS
love poetry, (which i love!) in particular,
"I carry your heart with me."

i cherish your sweet soul deep within me (i cherish
deep within me, your sweet soul.)

i imagine your smile (i, wear it) in the morning (i,
leave with it.)

keeping your smile with me at night (wherever you
are, i long to be)

i chance no loss of you. (without you i am lost to
chance.)

i hold your hand, my love. As do the stars, and
the moon. (the stars and the moon hold your
hand, cherishing and bathing your hand in exquisite
warm light.)

the world is this love, my love. (love is this love, my world.)

your stars are twinkling bright, (bright are your twinkling stars.)

you shine like the moon, it glows just like you. (Just like you, you shine, like the moon.)

This sensual press of your tender kiss, lingers, opening my heavens. (opening my heavens, this sensual, tender kiss lingers.)

I WHISPERED MY LOVE

I whispered my love
in subtle beats of my heart
missing his caress.
His absence unbearable
stark rhythms of loss.

But he wrote to me.
Love letters across oceans.
Professing such love
to be returned to me soon.
His heartbeats tracing my heart.

JUST FOR ONE MORE SWEET DAY

The mist is clinging to my clothes
My washing pulls and jerks against the breeze
The cold is deep within my skin, my bones
and in the threads of loneliness I bear.

In a field a digger cranks its jaws, it roars
Its jaws digging, deep
Plucking out mounds of mud
Excavated from this cold, red, earth.

Deep below on hills you loved
You rest, lost on this fateful day,
Mud slip slide, a year ago,
Caught, unable to be found.

No, all lies, you stand with me!
On this hilltop, every day in the breeze,
in each waking moment, in starlit trails,
in the breath of breaking dawn, by

moonlight's tender beams.

Two hearts like ours are bound
together forever.
Our magical vows kneel like
mountaintop promises.

I will never lose my love for you
I vow you this, my darling, I pledge.

So, this day, I unpeg little items of you.
Cold and rigid in my hand, I bring them in.
I hold your favourite shirt close.
Washed each year your scent anew.
I will bring this precious remnant of you in first.
Placing it in our wardrobe next to my warm clothes.

Wishing you here, my love, just now,
Just forever, just for one more sweet day.

LOVE, LIFE, WAR & FORGIVENESS

LOVE HAS NO AGE

Love has no age,
Eighteen, thirty-one,
Sixty?
Odd and even numbers.
Doesn't matter.
Even if a little unusual.

To be older
Or younger
Makes youngsters laugh.

One says:
I'd go out with a sixty-year-old!
Youngsters on a tram, poking fun.

Talking gibberish,
Getting wilder,
Things they say.

Just harmless goading,
But I know the truth,

Makes no odds.

Thirteen years,
Older,
Still together,
In love,
His soul age is the same,
As hers.

WAR TALK

After all that sweetness
Let's talk of love
A desire I have to do so.
Why not?
What else is there?
Love is it.
Simply that.

After all that sweetness
Let's talk of lust
A desire I have to do so.
Why not?
What else is there?
Lust is it.
Sometimes that.

After all that sweetness
Let's talk of war
No desire I have to do so.

Why not?
There is an ugliness in war
Love can't hide.

***

We met in the shelter
Bombs making us huddle closer
She was scared and unaware
An enemy was beside her

It was I who forgot war
Instead, I gazed upon her open mouth
an unlit cigarette dangling
Teasing me, to stare.

I imagined my tongue invading
Like a marauding soldier
Morals long forgotten
Lust fuelled by war.

My hardness grew with my shame
Screaming, stop! No voice to hear
Pulse quickening, she screamed,
"You disgust me."

Flicking her cigarette away

Distressed by my prying eyes.
She eased her body away.
Hands trembling, she lit a cigarette.

Its flame coloured, red hot.
Smouldering, my cheeks burned.
She dragged hard on the cigarette
Inviting me to stare again.

A GIRL AT A BAR

A girl at a bar,
solo gig, no rock band.
Watch her, wing it!
At just twenty years old
she is slim, smiles a lot.
A little nervous.
Makes us too.
Giggles in between
slow numbers, wants us to dance.
Her infectious joy smiles.

She has it. Her parents see it too.
talent,
voice,
good looks,
red lipstick,
sparkly outfit,
sex appeal.

Tears fill my eyes.
Longing for lost caresses

at the bar I order drinks.

See a man, alone.
Who might be game to join me,
I lick my lips.

The singer leaves.
I wish her well.
Youth, rekindled, farewell.

A NIGHT AWAY

A night away in a hotel
No thrills just possibilities
What about the pub next door?
Might find love.

I'd have a go
Try anything
For that illusive
Love.

World's End perhaps?
Burrowed away in a corner
Before last orders is called
If not, just be neighbourly.

Might I pat the dog?
Sitting quietly with his owners
Chance for a friendly chat at least
Don't knock it.

I could even join in open mic

Singing impromptu
Folk choruses in the pub next door
Banging on a drum.

Setting the music notes
To a whole new love affair
Which someone else will sing
Clapping as it ends.

GOTTA STICK TOGETHER, LADIES

Manchester to Edinburgh.

My mission was to find a vacant seat,
A sweet spot, what a treat!
Right by the luggage racks,
Opposite a guy who sits alone –
fact.
He scowls at me as I sit down,
How rude! An ignoramus - I frown.
His mouth turns to an obligatory smile.
But, not for me. Oh no! What a trial.

A girl squeezes beside him.
Pretty.
Foreign looking, slim.
French perhaps?
He drools, tongue lolling, his chins collapse,
Later, I hear about his heart issue,
Can't drink red bull, pass me a tissue!

So, he sups a Fanta orange instead,
Believes he can handle her - maybe bed,
Huh. Really? Such make believe!
Try not to lose more hair over it - please!

She then speaks, sounds kind of odd.
He sneaks closer, eyeing her up, what a sod,
Can't do enough for her.

Am I invisible? Fading to a blur.

A woman past her prime.
Don't believe it. I still have time.

Some men flirt and don't admit.

They're pathetically obvious - what a tit!

She is polite, a little shy,
Doesn't pay him much attention - or even try.

I offer to help her with her bag,
Rejects me, what a devilish drag!
She loses my womanly respect,
What can you expect?
Prefers a man's help - to mine,

Foolish Miss, why? I whine.

Two men long to help her - it's a sign.
A trolley service employee joins in - what a bind.
He proposes a solution and off he trots,
Ticking the company dot-to-dots,
Thanks, received, he pushes her luggage in,
Inventive space saving, his face grins.

He moves on happily, what fun!
Pulling out a pen she writes a pun,
Makes it look like it's all over and done.

Green cover, gold crocodile notebook - that's it,
Writing longhand, she muses and sits,
While I draft this poem out on my phone.
She writes hers down using a different tone.

Her opinion is at odds with mine.
But might be the same, that's also fine.
I swear I spot the word fuck.
Fucking men.
I hope so. Duck.
But somehow, I doubt it - no.
She is too young to understand.

What - a blow.

But one day she will, I believe it's true.

Until then! Gotta stick together, ladies. We must do!

IF FORGIVE IS A WORD
ON MY TONGUE

If forgive is a word on my tongue

A flutter in my heart

A stroke of your hair

I can't speak it yet

Or feel its beat

Or touch you

If forgive is a cruel memory

A deed you did

A wrong you done

Your regret and suffering I forgive.

STRANGERS IN LOVE

SILHOUETTES

She is fair and I am dark.
Slight and I am robust.

We fill out together.
Completing our silhouettes.

As we explore each other.
Strangers a moment ago.

Now lost, unable to fade away.
Because we kissed the deepness
of each other's shadows and stayed.

TAKING OUT THE TRASH

I see her but nothing changes.

Invisible, I'm just another nondescript
man walking by.

Until we share that burden of taking out the trash.

Bonding over rubbish.

It seems simpler to recall.

Our lost loves, now discarded,

like broken containers.

Our bodies, become vessels.

Her trash, a ripped stocking.

Which I tenderly peel off her.

Trembling she unbuttons my jeans.

SSH, TOUCH MY LIPS

Ssh, touch my lips she said
Drunken gibe at party
Her fingertip hovering
Inches away moving closer
Felt her breath upon my parted lips
We stood like that for ages
Poised knowing what would happen
Willing it wanting it
The kiss was slow building a beginning
But in its intensity intoxicating us
Momentum exquisite we arched closer
We forgot everything the party faded
Sensation growing tantalising
Two strangers lost to reason
Lips locked unexpectedly in love!

MY BOXER BOY

For a second, I fell in love.
With a stranger strutting in his boxer shorts
leaving nothing to the imagination.
He turned to do it all again.

Exiting the catwalk, he went, I to his boudoir.
We talked, I stalked, I left all animated.
Up close his face was as lively as his ass.

We met again, a second chance to see that...
twinkle beyond his eyes.
He had a wicked sense of humour.
Stripping down to his boxer shorts.
He catwalked for me, strutting his thing.
We ended up in a tangle of limbs
Me untangling his boxer shorts!

We never met again, my boxer boy and I.
He catwalked away to a new destination.
But he remains a fuzzy, warm memory in my heart.
The one that got away taking his

firm thighs with him.

I imagine him, muscles rippling across his chest.

The mirage he evokes, my precious
dream, he isn't shy!

He winks at me, as he poses, beckoning
me over, he smiles.

BEAUTIFUL STRANGERS
IN LOVE

You shuffled past head down absorbed
strumming your guitar.
Thinking of an excuse to get to know you
I lifted your chin and caught your gaze.
But speech evaded me embarrassment
making me glance down at my feet.

Placing your guitar down for a moment
you lifted my chin looking amused.
We locked eyes unsure what to do next.
You, my beautiful stranger, sidestepped to the left.
And I, his beautiful stranger,
sidestepped to the right.

We laughed.
This dance, our unexpected courtship ritual.
Brushing the hair from his face I
held his trembling hand.
He tucked a stray strand of my hair away too.

No words were spoken.

Our eyes and actions did the talking.
This language, the guitar chords of our love.

QUIRKY!

BAGPIPES, BUSKERS
AND RED BOOTS

The energetic bagpipe player leapt about.
Young girls were up dancing and foot tapping.
I liked the band's chat, their passion.

Even their jolly bagpipes.

Their name, no! Not so much.

Later, I spot a lone busker in Princes Street Gardens.
Dressed in cheesecloth playing old Cream songs.
Near him a girl listens and waits.

She is alone, staring ahead, smiling.

Her red cowboy boots bring back memories.

Of a pair l had long ago. Brown,
fancy, uncomfortable.
Hers are soft leather, calf length, the perfect colour.
I imagine them caressing her skin.
My skin. Her skin. My skin.

My heart longs for those lovely red boots!

Sighing. I groan. What a day to be in a hurry.
I am due elsewhere. How can it be?
Instead, I long to sit beside her on that park bench.
Striking up a conversation about those red boots.

Perhaps I could get a pair? Could I?

Instead that darn busker carries on singing.

He knows. Yes, he knows he will play a new song.
A different song. To alter the course of love.
He must.
To pause the soundtrack of his loneliness.

His reward will be. Will be. You guessed it!

To bring both her and those lovely red boots home.

PUCKERING UP FOR PASSION

In Manchester looking for a pub.

In the seedy dark,
Fag ends litter the floor,
Lovers entwine,
Pretending to hide.

Lips lock longingly,
Beseeching, see us kiss!
Transfixed,
I stop and stare,

Puckering up for passion.

Their kiss lingers lusciously.
Look at me!
It smacks.
The lovers disentangle, leave, resume.
Walking side-by-side.

Fading to ordinary,

Two unlikely exhibitionists,

Grey clothes hide their truth.

Pink lips tingling.
They disappear,
Merging into the throng.

Looking for another dirty spot.
To show-off,
Kiss.

TRAIN JOURNEY -
FAMILY MAN

He is all perfection.

Irritation.

His long legs stretch out blocking the aisle.

Unable to fit into the tight space on the train.

His large luggage is a burden.

A false rack deceives.

With its cruel optical illusion.

He is handsome, vocal, complaining.

His two teen daughters sit opposite,

Hair identically plaited.

One with freckles, like a cheetah.

The other's wearing pink headphones.

Both tune out their dad's moaning, or try to.

His wife says nothing. She's oceans away.

I can hardly see her. She might as well not be there.

He groans, witters on,
Talks to me, anyone, about the luggage,

Desperate for someone to hear him.

I don't reply. I don't know why.

He seems to accept this.
My ignoring him. His family ignore him too.

Listen, please! In silence, his desperation drips.

Like a leaky faucet needing repaired.

And yet. There is something about him.
A strangely erotic quality.
That draws my eyes towards him.
But - he has one tiny, immense flaw.
One, I've missed, completely.
Transfixed, I only noticed his fit body.
Long legs, chiselled jaw, tattoos on both hands.

An important item is long gone.

Teeth, a bite, both of which are missing.

How can he chew?

Or, run his tongue over his teeth.

His gums appear almost empty.
Except for two lonesome front molars.
Later, I learn, the rest are long gone too.
This leaves a huge gap for complaint.
Or does it?
Perhaps that's why his poor wife is silent!
Finding respite upon a faraway shore.

BEND IT LIKE A PRETZEL

Guys on a Piccadilly tram.
Overheard, their curious conversation.
One yawns, tired.
Need a rest tonight, mate, he pleads.

What no more? … Bend it like a pretzel?
The other guffaws.
Bend what? I muse confused…
My mind boggles, did I hear them right?

Did one bend and the other stand?
A new karma sutra,
Or is this just guys banter…
A new code for me to crack?

Listening some more… this time,
Toilet humour, need to pee gaffs,
A drunken night, no doubt,
Sexual shenanigans, or what?

With no context, I'll never know.

My curiosity gets me into trouble.

Twists my imagination, turns it,
Curls it, Pretzels it.

Off to Canal Street, next,
Can't see them lads,
Just a lot of people drinking,
Milling by sunning themselves.

Hoping for an opportunity,
To meet someone, or gossip,
Or at the very least,
Catch a Drag Queen show.

BLACKPOOL FUNNY GIRLS DRAG SHOW

Will I ride that spinning death
trap-
Or pop a penny in the well?
Make an illicit wish close my eyes
grip my thighs
real tight and
yell?

Secrets whispered carried afar.

The wind blows,
I run, my umbrella flaps.
Whips inside out.
It breaks - useless rubbish.
Perhaps chuck it, get shelter.
Leave the rides behind.
To venture to a Funny Girls, show?
Standing room only.
Or sneak a seat with a booth?

All this happening, before the after party.
Time to do the conga.
Gripping the girl in front I laugh.

My head somewhere in the gods.
But not too drunk to notice.
The drag queen who smiles at me.
I proffer her the broken glass.
The snapped off stem.
She takes from my hand.
With thanks given, respectfully.
I smile.

PUNK MUSIC BABE

She's for real!

My computer generated
AI punk Music
Babe.

black tattoos
adorn her
neck and arms.
her emerald
lips, a parted suggestion
that I may kiss her.

She's for real!

My computer generated
AI Punk Music
Babe.

bold eyes blink in shadows,
saucy salmon pink arch of eyebrows,

her unreal
luscious look
excites me.

She's for real!
My computer generated
AI Punk Music
Babe.

chunky headphones
fuchsia, today,
green tomorrow,
resting on her hair,
nestled close,
beside her,
partly shaven head.

She's for real!
My computer generated
AI Punk Music
Babe.

striking raven
blackest locks,
the meanest

greenest strands,
fall over one
slender shoulder,
free to flow unchecked.
She's for real!
My computer generated.
AI Punk Music
Babe.

She's almost mine!

I must
complete
her furtive
face. With one
spectacular, intense
stroke of genius!

She is - Isn't real?

My computer generated
AI Punk Music
Babe.

A daring dash of cheekbones
completes her

decadent look.
Followed by
a clusterfuck
of black tattoos.

But she's not mine!

She isn't real!

Has her own #Tag
@ AI
Wear a gold *

How much %
Creative
Imagination Is needed?
Goodbye. Babes!

TRAIN SECRETS - EDINBURGH TO GLASGOW

Edinburgh, an infamous Burke and Hare

Destination - a direct and cunning
route to my next crime…

I lost my train ticket, but the handsome
inspector didn't mind!

Naughty fellow! My sensuous smile
convinced him of my innocence.

Brilliant. He gave me his number. My
false smile aroused him.

Unwelcome, furtive hands brushed
mine. I should have crushed his.

Right then. Right now. But he moved away.

Growling with displeasure I crumpled
his note into a tight ball.

Hallelujah. I smiled, remembering
my shocking secret!

Tell someone? I didn't want to. Not likely.

Oh, Mr. Inspector, if only you knew!
You got off lightly.

Glorious, wicked thoughts kept me dreaming,
Lying next to his tempting body,

All tight, holding him ever so close...
Strangling him as he lay unsuspecting,
Gets rough, this handiwork, my unladylike deed.
Ordinarily, I never let them go.

Well dearie, I, Kill 'em. I Confess. I do!

POLE DANCING - SURPRISE!

The art of performing the splits
Whilst twirling on a pole
In skimpiest lingerie and high heels
Keeps her fit.
Winking, she smiles
as her long legs stretch up the pole.

Without a stocking snag,
Or a hair out of place,
Her silky contours flow,
Lips trembling.
She kisses the bare metal.

Surprise! A siren blows,
Dash! The firefighters dash,
One by one with zealous zeal,
All vanishing.
Sighing they slide down the same pole.

Fire men's hats bright and yellow,
Racing by they go, one by one,

In swift succession,
Forgetting everything.
Remembering only her sighs –
soft, sweet, serene.

Feeling her poignant presence,
Willing them to face their fears,
They imagine her fateful pose.
As she extends her kind hand.

They hold her burning body ever so tight.

SENSUAL SIGHS

VOYEUR WILL YOU?

She is mine and I am hers
Our secret to share
I do not regret these acts of serial...
Adultery.
Not until... I am caught.
A door opening, witness to my lust,
Angry voices, and half truths
Now alone again I debate...
Whether to tease open the door again.

The crack door ajar   a curious strip peephole
Intrigued by this view   the passing voyeur pauses
Temptations await   bed sheets
lay fresh, and untouched
Nakedness, glimpses   revealed as her towel slips
Soft belly exposed   a dance of gyrating curves
Hot hairdryer blasts   warm air to her luscious locks
Breasts all a tingle   her smooth
skin is yours to touch
Come and caress me   dare to push open my door!
Inhale my sweet scent   breathe

in my heady perfume

Lay down beside me   join me on these silken sheets

Untangle my dreams   towel dry my tumbling hair

Forget everything   discard the damn hairdryer

Blow me hot kisses   bring joy, passion, desire.

Become this naked   complete me
with your sweet love.

NATURE'S GODDESS

Nature's Goddess,
Wears a crystal encrusted crown,
Adorned with seductive Morganite,
And Ruby if the mood takes her.
In the forest, she awaits you.

The fullness of her lips,
Painted cherry red,
Such beauty in perfect symmetry,
Skin as white as silk.
Green the dress that adorns her.
In the forest she awaits you.

THE EAGLE

The eagle spreads its wings as you draw near.

Wind blows tempests in your hair
making the clouds blush pink.

Your rosy, red cheeks gleam, a solitary
tear spills from your eyes.

My fingertip captures its watery descent.

Lips part pink as you pull a juicy
cherry with your teeth.

I pluck it from your mouth savouring
its bittersweet flavour.

The sky shifts and clouds shuffle
pulling you towards me.

We gasp anticipating the touch of
rain on our bare shoulders.

The storm erupts and we collide as
thunder draws out our sighs.

Two forces of nature entwined.

The eagle soars,
becoming a moving speck in the distance.

SUNFLOWER PARAMOUR

Tilts her silken locks to the heady sunflower.
Breathes in its intoxicating arousing heat.
Closes her eyes and is deliciously empowered.
Tilts her silken locks to the heady sunflower.
Dreams of the sonorous voice of her paramour.
Her heart hiccups with a stolen, snatched beat.
Tilts her silken locks to the heady sunflower.
Breathes in its intoxicating arousing heat.

THE LUSTY WITCH IN ME

As I tap away
Conjuring stories
You distract me.
Plucking my attention away
Trailing kisses on my neck
We pretend I haven't noticed you.

It's a game we like to play.

As I lean back towards you
I choose a red font.
My lipstick matches its colour.
Your desire grows as bold.
Twirling my chair around
You kiss me.

It's a game we like to play.

With mounting urgency
I type random words.
Spaced apart like sweet kisses.

Laughing we draw apart.
You gasp.

Regarding me differently.

It's a game we like to play.

I have become a new character.
A wanton witch
My hair raven black
My eyes the richest gold
Curves to make you sigh.
Living in this forbidden story.

It's a game we like to play.

DEVIL'S TEMPTRESS

Dare

To smoke

My bright flame

Intense so hot

I daren't come close

To feel your heat is death

But without it will I die?

Plunging my hand in ice water

Like an addict I will try again

In eternity my heart burns for you

Flames lick enticing me closer to you

Devil's temptress bold and so daring

Willing me to hold you closer

Your fire burns, my pulse soars

Your breath lacerates me

Intense your bright heat

Moist lips burning

Desire

Heightens

Dies

KILLING ME WITH
YOUR SIGHS

(Acrostic poem with my page name, Kyrosmagica)

Killing me with your sighs
You hold me close, so close I fly
Right into the crystal heart of you
Ordinarily I close my eyes I do
Slip down your spine with my breath
Might kiss your collarbone, death
Arching closer goading my fate
Gripping you ever so tight I wait
I feel your excitement burning
Coming closer, shivering twirling
As I experience my exquisite unfurling

HUSH, SHE SAID

Hush, she said, a finger to his lips
Let my lingering kisses trail their path
Discovering the length and breadth of you
Hot like lava on your skin
A new territory discovered

Able arms will arch me in

This growing desire demands
my ardent attention
This fountain of energy
Builds in taut tempo beats
Dizzy with desire
Sweet as silk, she sighs
Growing swift as staccato breaths
Building with momentum
A high note sings
Its total release
Cradling them together until…
Spent, they sleep.

SILENT SIGHS

Long thigh length boots
I hear her coming.
Black hair as sleek as silk, I see.
High cheekbones aflame,
She staggers, strutting.
Silent sighs.
The biggest eyes.

I touch her neck. My finger lingers.
Circling sultry skin.
She smiles we kiss.
Forgetting breathing.
I lick, and lick, longingly.
Throaty sighs escape. You and I.

We tip over, fall. Laughing.
The grass our make do turf bed.
Boots and clothes discarded.
Naked skin exploring.
I feel myself respond. Penis hard.

The moon shines as we glide
Earth, body, skin. Awakening,
touch of fire, lips ablaze,
Passion flares, she, me
Ecstasy we crave.

Divine. Exquisite. Intensity.

We are two.
Becoming one, together her juicy petals dance,
Climaxing with the moist rain
As the grass shudders beneath us.

ABOUT ME POEMS

The best way to express a little about me
is to write a few concluding poems!

HAPPINESS

Happiness is not just you and me
It's family, and friends
Sunshine days
Mindfulness, tai chi
And the changing seasons.

Forest walks
Finding your childhood self
Collecting seashells
Exploring creative pursuits.

Could be art and photography
Loving rocks and crystals
Writing words and poetry
Reading much loved books.

Eating and drinking a glass, or two!
Travelling, discovering yourself
Making love and feeling magical.
Hugging and forever kissing.

Happiness is that smile, that laugh.
A love of and zest for life.
Happiness is this day. Your day.
Best shared with the ones you love.

LIVING IN THE MOMENT

Living in the moment the cock crows
announcing a new day.

Today, Majorca, tomorrow Portugal.

We live this life of travels, new experiences,
admiring each spectacular sunset.

Music strums the tunes of new adventures.
Wine tasting in a Mallorcan Bodega?

Talking to friends trying new foods,

Olives, local cheeses, nuts and dried fruit,

We remember Rui's BBQ fish at Fuseta,

The sea sparkles sublime with crystal blue waters.

In Parc National de Sandrago the ocean's
beauty is protected by cleansing algae.

In deeper waters near our hotel the evening
sea is deep, black and sleek as ink.

High winds bring stormy seas and high winds,

Whilst in Palma, a man exercises near the rocks!

We laugh as sprays of water soak us.

Remembering similar days in Cascais,

Sunshine smiles, storms, and rain bring laughter,

The cockerels and hens roam free

beside the families of feral cats.

Listening to the beat of our soul.

We discover new ways to live.

Keeping all our friends and dearest
ones in our hearts

we embrace the beauty of new lands.

THANK YOU

T hank you so much for reading. I hope you enjoyed this collection of sensual/love/life poems. Don't forget to review on the usual sites. As an independent author of poetry this really helps me and is especially important.

Please, dearest reader,
Write me a review, please do.
A few lines will do!

Thanking you in anticipation.

ACKNOWLEDGEMENTS

To the wonderful community of poets, authors, book reviewers, and readers, thanks to you all. And to my writing community, for their feedback and encouragement, on this project, my beta, and early readers: Sally Cronin, Debby Gies, Colleen Chesebro, Julia Sutton, Michelle Northwood, Ritu Bhathal, Richard Dee, D. L. Finn, Adele Marie Park, and always indebted to Colleen Chesebro for her encouraging me to write poetry with her Tanka Tuesday prompts. That's where it all began!

Some of the additional poems in this collection were originally written in response to the 365day poetry prompt challenge via **Melissa – Poetry of Me Md**, including:

Hot Shower Pounding Petals on My Skin, (onomatopoeia prompt suggestion via Donna Day)
Our Log Cabin Christmas Getaway, (winter related,) My First Glimpse of The Christmas
Tree, (Baccresieze,) My Honey Dearest My Sweetest You (primary colours, blue, yellow, red,)
Tangerine Dress, (word bank: tangerine, citrine, carnelian, crimson, coral, aubergine.) His

Girlfriend's Long White Coat, (Magic 9, 9 lines, rhyme scheme abacadaba) Just for One More Sweet Day, (prompt, lost) The Tree of Lost Love, (lost love,) The Universe is Ours, I whispered My Love, (Somonka poem,) Love Hidden in The Margins - If I were A Poem, (Prompt, If I were a poem.)Tribute poetry, Sunflower Paramour, (sensual using nature as stimuli, my prompt suggestion,) The Eagle, (sensual using nature as stimuli, my prompt suggestion.) Devil's Temptress, (Fire, Etheree followed by reverse Etheree,) Killing Me With Your Sighs, (Name Rhymed Acrostic) My Boxer Boy, Beautiful Stranger in Love, (love poem to a stranger,) and About Me section: Happiness Poem, (prompt suggestion via Stellar,) and Living in The Moment.

Two collaborative poems: Love Plucked, (myself and A. Lee Wells Poetry, Blooms of
Blossoming Bliss, (myself and Melissa, The Poetry of Me MD.)

Melissa: **Melissa, The Poetry of Me MD**

A. Lee Wells: **A. Lee Wells Poetry**

Sales of charity anthologies via Melissa.

The Endeavor Maiden Voyage, The 365 Challenge Compendium Volume 1via Lulu.

The Endeavor Smooth Sailing, The 365 Challenge Compedium Volume 2 via Lulu.

Dining on Poetry was inspired by themes from the anthology which I released during lockdown: This Is Lockdown.

If Forgive Is A Word On My Tongue – was written in response to the following forgiveness prompt challenge posted by Victor Herrera

https://www.facebook.com/
ThoseMeaningfulWords.Official

ALSO BY M J MALLON

*Next Chapter Publishing
YA Fantasy series, The
Curse of Time*

*For details of publications
please visit:* **https://
www.nextchapter.pub/
authors/mj-mallon**

Kyrosmagica Publishing

Poetry and Flash Fiction: Do What You Love:
**https://www.amazon.co.uk/gp/product/
B0BKLC9DYY/**
Poetry and Flash Fiction: The Hedge Witch and The
Musical Poet: **https://bookstoread/u/mv1oev**
Poetry, Prose & Photography: Mr. Sagittarius:
http://mybook.to/MrSagittarius

Pandemic Poetry: Lockdown Innit Poems About
Absurdity
Pandemic Anthology: This IsLockdown

Available on Amazon kindle, Kindle unlimited

and paperback.

Short Stories in Anthologies:
Wordcrafter anthologies
Midnight Roost compiled by Kaye Lynn Booth
"The Cull," (Short Story)
Bestselling horror compilations
Nightmareland compiled by Dan Alatorre
"Scrabble Boy" (Short Story)
Spellbound compiled by Dan Alatorre
"The Twisted Sisters" (Short Story)
Wings of Fire compiled by Dan Alatorre
"The Great Pottoo" (Short Story)
Ghostly Rites 2019 compiled by Claire Plaisted
"Dexter's Creepy Caverns" (Short Story)
Ghostly Rites 2020 compiled by Claire Plaisted
"No. 1 Coven Lane" (Short Story)

For all my publications and contributions to anthologies, (including charity anthologies, 100 Ways to Write a Book, Alex Pearl, in aid of Pen International,) please refer to my Author Blog:

https://mjmallon.com **and my Amazon Author Page:**

https://www.amazon.co.uk/M-J-Mallon/e/ B074CGNK4L/

Twitter: @Marjorie_Mallon and @curseof_time
Goodreads: https://www.goodreads.com/author/ show/17064826.M_J_Mallon
Facebook: https://www.facebook.com/ mjmallonauthor/

Instagram: https://www.instagram.com/
mjmallonauthor/
Tik Tok: M J Mallon (@mjmallonauthor) TikTok |
Watch M J Mallon's

Bookstagram: M J Mallon (Marjorie Mallon)
(@mjm_reviews) · Instagram photos and videos
Bookbub: https://www.bookbub.com/
authors/m-j-mallon